The Swiss Family Robinson

Johann Wyss

Simplified by D K Swan
and Michael West

Illustrated by Mark Peppé

Longman

Addison Wesley Longman Limited,
Edinburgh Gate, Harlow,
Essex CM20 2JE, England
and Associated Companies throughout the world.

This simplified edition © Longman Group UK Limited 1988

First published 1988
Ninth impression 1996

ISBN 0-582-54157-3

Set in 10/13 point Linotron 202 Versailles
Printed in China
GCC/09

Acknowledgements

The cover background is a wallpaper design called NUAGE,
courtesy of Osborne and Little plc.

Stage 3: 1300 word vocabulary

Please look under *New words* at the back of this book
for explanations of words outside this stage.

Contents

Introduction

Johann Rudolph Wyss (1782–1830) was a professor in Berne in Switzerland. He was well known as a student of folklore – the special national or group beliefs, customs, etc, that have been passed from parents to children for hundreds of years. But he is more widely remembered as the man who gave the world *The Swiss Family Robinson* in 1812. This novel was his own work, but it began as an uncompleted story by his father, Johann David Wyss.

Wyss took the idea for *The Swiss Family Robinson* from Daniel Defoe's *Robinson Crusoe*, so we had better look at Defoe's novel first in this Introduction.

The idea for *Robinson Crusoe* came from the real adventures of Alexander Selkirk. Selkirk quarrelled with the captain on his ship, and was put on to the island of Juan Fernandez in 1704. He was rescued when another ship visited the island in 1709. Daniel Defoe took Alexander Selkirk's story and added descriptions and events of his own. He didn't pretend that *Robinson Crusoe* (1719) was a true story, though many people believed it was. The story-telling was so like a real-life account that it seemed completely true. Remember that the novel, as a form of literature, didn't appear in England until about 1740. Defoe's story has Robinson Crusoe describing very carefully how he used the things he saved from the ship and the things he found on the island. He also describes his fight to keep command of his own mind during the long years alone on the island. Exciting moments are his discovery of a footmark in the sand, his seeing a group of man-eating savages visiting the island, and his saving from them the man he calls Friday, who becomes his servant.

Robinson Crusoe was not written to teach any special lessons. Wyss's *The Swiss Family Robinson* was different. The idea was to show a family working together in perfect family love through every kind of difficulty. The father, who is the narrator (the person who tells the story), teaches his sons lessons that the readers ought to learn. Most of all, they must learn the value of patience, hard work and helping each other. There is a great deal of religious teaching in the original very long (two volumes) book, but modern editions usually shorten the story and keep the more exciting and adventurous parts.

At the time of the story, ships often carried such birds and animals as hens, ducks, pigs, sheep, cows, goats and donkeys. Some of these were owned by passengers who were on their way to settle in newly discovered countries. Some were to supply fresh food on long voyages because, as we must remember, the sailing ships of the time were slow, and they had no canned food and certainly no form of cold storage.

We may think the Swiss family were very lucky to find on one small island all the animals, plants and other things they used. Again there is something we must remember: even as late as 1812 there was very little known about many parts of the world. James Cook's voyages of discovery in the South Pacific were made between 1768 and 1779. Wyss must have read about them, but there was still a great deal to be learnt about the places whose coasts Cook visited and other places which had not yet been discovered. The first readers of this book would not have been at all surprised about the great number of different things found on the island.

Although we may find it harder than the first readers to believe in the island, *The Swiss Family Robinson* is still an interesting and exciting story about the way people can build their lives in a strange and difficult place.

Chapter 1
Ship on the rocks

The storm had lasted for six days. The captain did not know where he was. All those in the ship believed that their lives would be lost.

My wife and my four young sons gathered close to me.

"My dear children," I said, "God can save us."

Then, above the noise of the storm, I heard a cry: "Land! Land!" The ship struck the rocks.

The captain cried, "There's no hope now. Let down the boats."

"No hope!" cried the children.

"Be brave, my boys," I said. "The land isn't far off. This is one of the many small islands in this part of the world. I've seen them on the map. God will show us a way of saving ourselves. I'll go up and see what can be done."

I went up and saw that all the boats were in the sea and all the men had left the ship. They had gone away in the boats and forgotten us!

Then I looked towards the land. The front part of the ship was held up between two rocks so that it was above the water.

I went back to my family. "It's all right," I said. "Part of the ship is above the water. Tomorrow the waves will have gone down and we'll be able to reach the land."

Night came. My wife prepared a meal and the boys went to bed, but my wife and I kept watch.

Day came. There was less wind and the waves were going down. The sky was clear and the land was not far off.

"Now," I said, "let's go round the ship and see what we

can find to help us to reach the land. Then we'll meet here, bringing anything useful that we have found."

I went to the store-room to see what food and water we had. Fritz, the eldest boy, brought back guns and gunpowder and shot. My second son, Ernest, found a box of tools – a hammer, a lot of nails, saws, a big knife, and some small knives – and some other things. The box was very heavy but Fritz helped him to carry it.

My third son, Jack, opened the door of the captain's room and two big dogs jumped out at him. They were quite friendly and he led them along.

Then my wife came and told me what she and Francis, my youngest son, had found. "We have found a cow, a donkey, two goats, a pig, two sheep, and some hens and some ducks."

I said, "All those things will be useful – but not the dogs. They'll eat too much."

"But, father," said Jack, "they'll help us in catching animals for food when we reach the land."

"Yes," I said, "but we haven't yet reached the land. We must think of a way of doing it. We must make a boat. Let's get some barrels and some pieces of wood."

So we set to work and made a boat. It was very heavy. We made a mast and a sail, and we found some oars.

"We'll put up the mast when the boat's in the water," I said.

"But how will we get it into the water?" asked Fritz.

"We must put rollers under it. Then it will roll along and go into the sea."

At last everything was ready.

I fixed a long rope to our boat and tied the other end to the ship so that our boat would not be carried away.

Then we had a meal and we all slept peacefully.

2

Chapter 2
The island

We were all awake at sunrise. I called the children together and said, "We must first feed the animals. I hope we'll be able to come back and bring them later. Now gather together everything that will be useful to us."

We took guns and powder and shot. Each carried a bag full of food. We took some cooking pots, the hammer, saw, nails, knives, axes, and we brought sailcloth to make a tent and a sail for the boat. The hens seemed sad at being left, so we brought them with us. "The ducks and the dogs," I said, "can swim behind the boat."

At the last minute my wife came, carrying a big bag. I did not ask what was in it.

At first the boat turned round and round, but after a time I found the way to make it go towards the land.

"Look," cried Fritz as we came nearer the shore, "Look: those are coconuts. We shall have coconuts to eat."

The ducks were swimming towards a little bay.

"They know the best place to land," I said, "so I'll follow them." They led us to the mouth of a stream which flowed into a little bay.

The two elder boys jumped on to the land, then helped Francis to follow them.

Then we began to bring the things from the boat. We set the hens free. Then I cut some long branches from the trees and fixed them in the ground and I put the sailcloth over them and made a tent.

"Now," I said to the children, "go and bring some dry grass for our beds." While they were doing this I got some big stones and made a place for our fire. I soon made a good fire, using dry wood which had been thrown up on the shore. My wife got a pot of water from the stream and put it on the fire. Then, helped by little Francis, she began to cook a meal.

Fritz took a gun and set off along the riverbank. Ernest went to the right along the shore and Jack went to the left to get shellfish. I went to carry more things from the boat to the land. Suddenly I heard Jack shouting. I took an axe and ran to help him. I found him standing in water up to his knees.

"Come here, father," he shouted. "Come quickly. I've caught something really big!"

"All right," I said, "bring it here."

"I can't. It has caught me."

I laughed. Then I struck the lobster with my axe and set Jack free. It had caught only his clothing, so he was not hurt.

"Well," I said, "Jack is the first boy who has found something that we can eat."

Just then Ernest came. "I've found some things that are good to eat, but I need help in getting them."

"What are they?"

"Shellfish. But I need help because they are stuck hard to the rocks. We'll get them later, after our meal."

"The food is ready," said my wife, "but we ought to wait for Fritz."

She looked at the pot of food. "How shall we eat it? We can't put our hands in: we can't take out the liquid with a knife! We need spoons, but we haven't got any spoons!"

"If we had coconuts we could cut them in half and use them."

4

"We could do that if we had coconuts, but we haven't."

"We have shells!" said Ernest. "Or we shall have if you'll come and help me to get them."

So Jack and Ernest went to get shellfish.

Soon after this Fritz came. He was looking sad.

"Didn't you find anything?" I asked.

"Ah!" he said sadly.

"Oh, he has!" cried Francis, who had gone behind Fritz. "He's hiding it behind his back."

Then Fritz laughed and showed what he had got.

"What is it?" he said. "It looks rather like a pig, but it isn't a pig. I saw it moving in the grass. Sometimes it was digging to get food out of the ground, and sometimes it sat up and seemed to be washing its face."

Ernest came back, followed by Jack, bringing shellfish.

"Let me see it," said Ernest. "Yes, yes, I think I've seen a picture of it in a book. It isn't really like a pig: its teeth are different and its skin is softer. I think it's an animal called an agouti."

"Ernest is right," I said. "It *is* an agouti. It lives in holes in trees: it's very good to eat."

Jack was trying to open a shellfish with a knife.

"I can't do it!" he said. "I can't open it."

"Put the shellfish near the hot fire," I said, "and they'll open without your help."

So we sat down to our meal. First we ate the shellfish so as to use the shells as spoons for the other food.

"But we haven't got any plates!" said my wife.

"I have a plate," said Ernest, showing a very big shell that he had found on the shore. "There are lots of these shells where I found this one."

"Then why," I asked, "didn't you think of others and bring plates for all of us? Give that shell to the dogs and eat out of the pot like the rest of us."

The dogs, which the children had named Turk and Flora, finished their meal very quickly but were still hungry. While we were eating they began to pull pieces off the agouti. Fritz saw this and was very angry. He hit the dogs with his gun: he hit them so hard that he broke part of the gun.

"Fritz," I said, "you are the oldest and the other boys watch what you do and do the same. You have taught them to be angry without reason and to hurt animals which meant no wrong."

"I'm sorry, father. Forgive me."

"Tell the dogs that you are sorry and ask their forgiveness."

Fritz took a piece of bread in each hand and was soon back, leading the two dogs behind him.

The sun was going down when we finished our meal. Then my wife opened the bag that she had brought from the ship and began to throw handfuls of corn to the hens. I stopped her.

"I'm very glad that you have brought the corn. That's very good. But we mustn't give it to the hens. We must use it as seed and grow corn to make bread. The hens can have other food."

The hens went up on the top of the tent. The ducks went in among the tall grasses on the edge of the stream. We loaded our guns and laid them at our sides. Then we said our evening prayers and went into the tent.

Chapter 3
The baby monkey

We woke up very early, the hens and the ducks woke us up.

"The first thing to do," I said, "is to see if any of the seamen from the ship have reached the land."

"We needn't all go," said my wife. "You take Fritz. I'll stay here with the others."

"Yes," I answered, "I'll take Turk with us, and Flora can stay with you."

My wife gave us bags of food to take with us and we set out. We went along the sea-shore looking for the marks of feet in the sand, but we found none.

Fritz had brought one of the other guns, as he had broken his.

"Shall I fire the gun? If they are near, they'll hear it and come to us."

"No!" I said. "Others might hear it. There may be wild men on the island, and it would be dangerous to let them know we are here."

We turned away from the shore and, after going about a mile we came to a little wood. At every step we saw some new and beautiful plant.

"What is this strange plant," said Fritz, "with these big things growing on it?"

"Ah," I said, "those are very useful. They are gourds."

We took some of the gourds and cut them open.

"Now we must take out the soft inside and leave the shell to dry in the sun. Then we can make spoons and plates and cooking pots. Men who have no iron or other metal make these things out of gourds."

"I don't understand how a cooking pot can be made from a gourd. If you put it on the fire, it'll burn."

"Ah," I said, "but they don't put it on the fire. They fill the gourd with water and then put hot stones into the water and so make the water boil."

We opened a number of gourds and cut plates and spoons and pots from them, and put them in the sun. We marked the place carefully so we could come back and get them later when they were dry.

We went on and came to some land covered with very tall grasses, growing high above our heads.

"Now where," I thought, "have I seen such grasses? Was it in a picture?"

We had to cut our way through the grasses. My hands became very sticky. I put a hand to my mouth, then I remembered!

"Come here, Fritz. Cut open one of these grasses and put the soft inside part in your mouth."

He did so. "Oh!" he said. "It's sweet. Like sugar!"

"It *is* sugar," I answered. "This is sugar cane, the plant from which we get sugar. Let's take some of these back with us. The others will be very pleased and surprised."

We went on and saw in front of us a lot of coconut trees. As we came nearer we saw a lot of monkeys on the ground near the trees. But they saw us and ran up into the trees making angry noises at us.

Fritz raised his gun.

"Stop!" I cried. "Why do you want to kill one of those monkeys?"

"Because they are making nasty, angry noises at us. They are nasty, useless things."

"Or perhaps they're laughing at you. Why do you

become so angry because you are being laughed at? They are right to laugh at an angry boy – and they aren't useless."

"How can you make a monkey useful?" said Fritz.

I gathered some stones and threw them at the monkeys, and they threw down coconuts at me.

"There!" I said, gathering up some of the coconuts to carry home. "An angry monkey can be quite useful."

"More useful than an angry boy?" said Fritz. "But I'm not angry now. Let me carry the coconuts."

As we came to some more coconut trees, the dog, Turk, ran on in front. We heard cries of pain and angry cries from the monkeys up in the trees. As we came nearer we saw that Turk had caught one of the monkeys.

Fritz ran forward to save it, but it was too late; the monkey was dead. Its young one was not far away: it was in the grass crying out in fear. Then a very strange thing happened. As soon as the baby monkey saw Fritz it jumped on his back and held on to his hair.

"Take it off! Take it off!" cried Fritz.

I laughed. "It has lost its mother and so it has taken you as its father. Yes, I can see how like its father it is!"

I gently took the monkey off Fritz's back and held it in my arms like a baby.

"Well, what shall we do with it?" I asked.

"Let me take it home," cried Fritz. "I'll get milk for it from the cow in the ship, and soon it'll learn to find food for itself ... Now, Turk," he said, "you killed the poor baby's mother; you must help me to be a father to it. I shall teach it to ride on your back."

My wife and the three boys saw us coming and ran out to meet us. They were very pleased to see the little monkey.

The monkeys throw coconuts at us

"What are those sticks?" they asked.

"They are for you to eat," said Fritz.

When we reached the tent we found a very good meal waiting for us. Several sorts of fish and a bird were cooking over the fire. Francis had caught the fish and Ernest had caught the bird.

"I don't know what bird it is, but it was so foolish that it let me come close and I hit it with my stick."

The fish was very nice, but we didn't like the taste of Ernest's bird: it tasted of fish.

The sun was setting when we finished our meal. The hens went up on to the top of the tent, and the ducks went into the grass near the stream. Fritz took the little monkey to bed with him.

Chapter 4
Back to the ship

As soon as I awoke I said to my wife, "There are so many things to be done that it's difficult to know which to do first."

"The first thing to do," she said, "is to go and bring those animals from the ship. You and Fritz go. The rest of us will look for a place to build a home."

I said to her, "We must stay on the ship all night. Tell Ernest to climb up that high tree and tie a piece of cloth there as a flag. If there is any danger, pull the flag down."

"You must put up a light in the ship," said my wife, "then I'll know that you have got there safely."

"All right," I answered.

We reached the ship quite easily.

The animals were in good health and had enough food.

I put up a light as I had promised my wife, then we had some food and went to sleep.

We woke very early next morning and spent some time gathering together things which would be useful to us on the island.

"We must have plenty of gunpowder and shot," said Fritz, "so that we will be safe against wild animals and any enemies. Later on we shall need ..."

"We must think of the present," I said. "What do we need now, for these next few days or weeks? We must take more sailcloth to help us to make a home, and we must think of food. What food is there on the ship?"

"I've seen a barrel of butter," said Fritz, "and there's the ship's bread, and salt meat – if it isn't spoilt by sea water.

But what will we do when the bread's used up and the butter's bad?"

"Let us think of the present time," I said. "We have enough troubles to think of without thinking of troubles which may come later. Perhaps a ship will come and take us away."

But I was wrong. People should always be prepared for whatever may come. So we made some foolish mistakes and did not bring back things that we badly needed later. These mistakes might have cost us our lives.

Gathering together these things filled the day and we had to spend a second night on the ship.

We woke up late next morning.

Fritz made ready some breakfast. I found the captain's telescope and through it I could see my wife come out of the tent and look towards the ship. I took down the light and put up a white flag to show that we were all right.

"Now, Fritz," I said, as we sat at breakfast, "how can we take those animals to the land?"

"We can't put them on the boat," he said. "They would be too heavy. Can we make another boat? . . . No, it would be far too big. What can we do? The pig can swim, but the cow and the sheep and the goats can't swim so far, nor the donkey."

"No," I said, "we can't make a boat big enough. There are a lot of barrels on the ship – enough for such a boat, but it would take too long to make one."

"Barrels!" cried Fritz. "Let's make each animal its own boat. Let us tie barrels on the animals to hold them up in the water and pull them behind the boat!"

"Well," I said, "that may be possible. Let's try first with one animal and see if it can be done."

We fixed a barrel on each side of a sheep and put it into the sea. It went down, down ... I thought it would never come up! Then at last I saw its head above the water and it began to swim. When it was tired, it stopped swimming and stayed there, held up by the barrels.

Fritz jumped down into the sea and tied a rope to the sheep and so we brought it back into the ship. We worked very hard and for a time thought that it would not be possible. The pig and the donkey were the most difficult.

"Perhaps we should leave them," said Fritz. "The cow and the goats are what we need most."

We tied barrels to the cow and the goats, and then we tried again to do the pig and the donkey. The donkey seemed to understand, but the pig gave us a lot of trouble.

"The pig is very fat," said Fritz: "perhaps its fat will keep it up on the water; and pigs are good swimmers." So we did not tie barrels to the pig.

So at last we got all the animals into the water. We gathered up the ropes to pull them if they needed help. We got into the boat and put up the sail.

There was a strong wind and we could soon see the little bay. When we reached the shore, I cut the ropes of the animals and they came up on to the shore, glad to be set free from their barrels.

My wife and the boys came running to meet us.

My wife was surprised to see all the animals – even the pig – brought safely to the land.

"How did you think of this way of doing it?" she asked.

"I didn't think of it," I answered. "I couldn't see any way of doing it. This was Fritz's plan."

Chapter 5
Finding a place for a home

"What did you do, my dear, while Fritz and I were on the ship?" I asked.

"I found a place for our new home," said my wife. "The heat in the tent was more than we could bear, and there are no trees here to sit under. So Ernest and Jack took their guns, and we carried with us enough food for the day. The two dogs came too. We came to a small river and crossed it on stones. Then we went on and reached some high ground and were surprised at the beauty of the country. From there I could see a small group of trees in the distance. We went on, and at last came to the trees. There were only ten or twelve trees, but they were the biggest I have ever seen. We stopped and ate our dinner there. It seemed to me the perfect place to live in. There! Now you know my story! I went to look for a new place to live in and I found one. If you really want to please me, promise we'll go there tomorrow and make a home for ourselves in one of those giant trees."

"What!" I said, laughing. "*In* a tree? A house in a tree! We might perhaps live under a tree, but how would we get up into the tree? Fly?"

"You may laugh if you wish, but I am quite sure we could build a small hut among the branches, with a way of getting up to it."

"Well," I said, "we'll all go and see the place tomorrow and think about what we can do."

Chapter 6
Going to our new home

During the night I had thought over what my wife had said, and as we sat at breakfast next day I said, "Yes, we'll go and live in that place that you saw on the other side of the river." I turned to the boys and said, "Now, what's the first thing we must do?"

"I know!" said Jack. "We must move the tent there and then take all our things, and then take the animals."

"What do you think, Fritz?"

"That place is on the other side of the river. Mother and Ernest and Jack and Francis went across on stones. But the cow and donkey and pig can't cross on those stones and we can't carry our things across the water."

"Well, what's the first thing we must do?"

"We must build a bridge. That's the first thing, isn't it?"

"No," said Ernest. "The first thing is to go out to the ship and bring wood to build the bridge with."

"We don't have to do that," said Jack, "because I saw lots of wood on the shore where that lobster caught me. The sea had carried it there from the ship, and there will be more there now."

"Good boy!" I said. "Let's go and see what we can find."

Jack was right. We found plenty of wood. We tied together the big pieces which would be useful to us and pulled them to the mouth of the stream. Then we got the donkey and with its help pulled the pieces of wood up the stream and on to the land where we wanted to build our bridge.

With difficulty we laid three long pieces across the river, then we nailed boards across them. It was very hard work and we all slept heavily that night. The next morning, we got up early and began preparing for our journey.

We put our pots and our food and all our small things into bags and hung them one on each side of the cow and the donkey. We put little bags on the goats, but we couldn't make the pig carry anything. We put Francis on the back of the donkey so that it could not run away. The boys and I carried our bed coverings and all that we would need for the first few days in our new home.

When we were all ready, my wife said, "We can't leave the hens here, or we shall lose them all."

Fritz and Ernest then began running about trying to catch the hens. They could not catch one!

"I'll show you how to do it," my wife said.

She threw a little food on the ground: all the hens ran to it. Then she threw some more inside the tent and they all went inside the tent. While they were eating she shut the opening.

"Now, Jack, you go into the tent. Catch the birds and hand them out to us. We'll tie their legs and put them in a basket on the cow's back."

At last we were ready to start. We put all the rest of our things inside the tent and closed it up carefully.

Fritz and my wife marched in front. Then came the cow and the donkey with Francis sitting on its back; then the goats led by Jack. The monkey rode on the goat from which he got his milk. After him came Ernest and the sheep, and I came last. The dogs ran round helping to keep us all in line.

The pig did not want to come with us, so we left it behind.

17

When we reached the bridge, the pig joined us. When it saw us going away, it came running after us making angry noises.

We crossed the bridge carefully, one at a time. I was afraid that the weight of the cow might break it, so the donkey went first. The bridge was all right, so the cow went next, and then the rest followed: but not the pig! Oh, no! The pig would not go on to the bridge. We tried to drive it; but no! Then, when we had all got across, the pig swam across and came after us.

So we came to the place where our new home was to be.

"What wonderful trees!" said Fritz. "How high they are!"

"Yes," I said, "I didn't think they were as big as this. This is a very good place. If we could climb one of those trees and make a house there, we would be safe from all wild animals."

We tied up the animals so that they could not wander away – but not the pig. The pig lay down and slept.

We set the hens free and they flew up into the trees. My wife had started a fire and cooked a meal for us.

Chapter 7
The rope ladder

When the meal was finished, I said, "We must sleep on the ground tonight, because I can't see how we can get up into a tree this evening."

Then I went to the shore with Fritz and Ernest to find the things needed to make a ladder. The shore was covered with pieces of wood of all sizes, carried there from the ship by the waves.

"It would be difficult to make a ladder out of these pieces of wood," said Fritz, "and it would be very heavy."

"Look at those very tall thick plants there!" cried Ernest, "they're just what we need! Bamboo!"

I cut some bamboo into pieces about two metres long and tied them together so I could carry them. Then I cut some straight sticks. I said, "With this bamboo I can make a bow, and I can make arrows from these sticks."

We came back to the biggest tree carrying the pieces of bamboo and put them down on the ground.

"That great branch is about ten metres high." I said. "We have over twenty metres of thick rope, a longer piece of thin rope and a lot of string. Now we'll lay out two long pieces of rope on the ground and we'll cut pieces of bamboo half a metre long. Fritz, you cut the pieces, Ernest will help me to lay out the rope."

So we set to work.

"Now," I said, "we must fix cross-pieces of bamboo into the rope to make steps. Then we'll have a rope ladder."

We worked very hard and after some hours our ladder was ready. Then I made a bow from a piece of bamboo.

"Ernest," I said, "get some feathers and make arrows

from these sticks. Put a big nail on one end and feathers on the other."

"Oh!" cried Jack. "A bow and arrows! What are you going to do with them? Let me play with them!"

"I'm not making a plaything, Jack. I'm going to shoot with this. But soon you shall all have bows and arrows because we must be careful with our gunpowder. When this gunpowder is used up we can't get any more. And, if there are wild and dangerous men on the island, we shall need our gunpowder for fighting against them."

When the bow and arrows were ready, I tied a long piece of string to an arrow and shot the arrow up, over the branch, and it came down on the other side, carrying the string with it.

"Now we will tie thin rope to the string and pull the rope over the branch."

"Ah!" said Ernest, who was always quick to understand, "then you'll tie the rope ladder to this light rope and pull that up on to the branch. Then you'll hold it there with the light rope while someone climbs up and fixes it on the branch."

"Yes," I said. "You go up, because you are smaller than Fritz and I don't think Jack can fix the ladder well enough."

Soon the ladder was fixed on the branch.

"That's a good day's work," I said. "Now we must tie up the animals and we'll sleep at the foot of the tree. Tomorrow we'll begin to build our Tree House."

"Look!" said Jack. "Our rope ladder is being used already!"

I looked: the hens had found a comfortable place, one on each step.

I lit a big fire to keep away dangerous animals, and decided to stay awake and keep watch.

The hens on our new rope ladder

21

Chapter 8
Building the Tree House

I was very restless at first: I felt that we were not in a very safe place. I heard a strange sound ... No! that was only the falling of leaves from the tree. The fire was getting low ... what were those shadows? Was that some beast moving nearer? ... nearer? I got up and put more wood on the fire. At last I felt safer and went to sleep.

It was daylight when I awoke. All the others were awake already. We had breakfast, then we set to work again.

·My wife milked the cow, and then went down to the shore with Ernest, Jack and Francis and the donkey. They went to get the wood that we would need for building the house.

Fritz and I climbed up the ladder into the tree, so as to plan our house.

"These branches," I said, "are thick and close together and they come out straight from the tree. The floor of the house can be here, and the tree will be one of the walls."

Fritz looked up and said, "Those branches higher up will hold up the roof. What sort of roof?"

"We'll put a sail over those branches and bring it down to the floor on two sides."

That, as you will hear later, was a great mistake. How foolish I was! But at the time Fritz and I were very pleased with our simple plans.

"This fourth side," I said, "will be open. We can look out from there, and perhaps we'll make a place where we can sit outside in the daytime."

"It will be a beautiful house!" said Fritz .... "What a

long time they are taking to bring the wood!"

At last my wife and Ernest appeared with the donkey pulling along a great load of wood. More wood was tied on its back and Francis was sitting on top of that.

They unloaded the wood and went back for more.

"How shall we get it up here?" said Fritz. "Shall I carry it up the ladder?"

"We must pull it up."

"With a wheel," said Fritz, "a wheel for pulling things up. What's the word?"

"A pulley."

"Yes! Yes! A pulley! Where did I see a pulley? It was in Ernest's box of tools."

Fritz found the pulley: we tied it to a branch and pulled up the pieces of wood. My wife and Ernest made two more journeys to the shore and then Ernest stayed and tied pieces of wood on the rope, and Fritz pulled them up. I went on making the floor while my wife prepared a meal.

When evening came the floor was finished, and we hung our sailcloth over the higher branches and nailed it down to the floor on two sides. On the fourth side we had a good look-out over the country round us and plenty of cool air could come into the house.

Fritz and I climbed down the ladder.

"There!" I said. "Our house is finished." I saw that there were some pieces of wood left.

"We'll make a table and some chairs from these tomorrow."

My wife had cooked a bird shot by Ernest on his way to bring wood. It was a very old bird and it tasted of fish, but we were very hungry.

We lit a fire to keep wild beasts away from our animals,

then I said: "Tonight we'll sleep in our new house."

The two older boys went quickly up the ladder carrying their bedding. My wife was rather afraid of climbing the ladder, but she reached the top safely. Then I took Francis on my back. I untied the ladder from the posts in the ground. I climbed up and pulled the ladder up after me.

"Now we are quite safe in our Tree House," said Jack. "Nothing can climb up here!"

"Oh!" cried Fritz. "Where's the monkey?"

"There!" said Ernest, pointing to Fritz's bed. "Nothing else can climb up here, but a monkey can climb up anywhere!"

I kept my gun by my side because I was still not quite sure that the animals were safe. But the night passed quietly.

Chapter 9
Back to the tent

After breakfast Fritz and I set to work to make a table from some of the rest of the wood.

Suddenly we heard a loud BANG and a small bird fell almost at our feet.

"That was a good shot!" said Ernest, coming to pick it up.

"It was *not* good," I said. "It's very bad to waste gunpowder in that way. We can use the guns to shoot large beasts for food, but for birds and small animals we must use bows and arrows. Look at the bow and arrow that I have made, Ernest, and try to make better ones – and learn to use them."

When midday came we put some barrels round and were ready to eat our first dinner sitting up round a table.

"Where are Ernest and Jack?" said my wife.

"Let's begin our meal. If they come late they'll get no dinner."

"Something may have happened to them," said my wife. "Some wild animal may have caught them. I can't eat if I don't know where they are."

We waited.

"I'm sure nothing has happened to them," I said at last. "They're young and foolish and don't notice the time. Put the food on the table."

Just as my wife did this, Ernest and Jack appeared, carrying bows and arrows.

"Look!" said Jack, before I could speak, and he held out a very small bird that he had shot with an arrow. "And look what Ernest has got! – A rabbit!"

It was a very small animal rather like a rabbit.

"I'm very pleased with what you have done, but I'm angry at your lateness. Your mother has been afraid that something had happened to you. Sit down and eat your dinner."

We had only meat and some bread for dinner. The bread was very hard and the meat was an animal that I had shot yesterday.

"I left some things at the tent," said my wife. "If we get them, I can give you a better dinner. And the ducks are still there."

We set out. The dogs went in front: the little monkey was riding on Turk's back. Then came Fritz, and Ernest and Jack with their bows and arrows. My wife and Francis and I came last. I carried a bag in which to bring back salt for our food.

As we went along the shore I saw that there was still a great deal of wood there, and I noticed two long pieces, just the same size and shape, both turned up at one end.

"Now where," I thought, "have I seen pieces of wood shaped like that? Ah! I remember! In Switzerland, of course!"

We reached the tent and found everything as we had left it. Everyone went to look for the things they wanted. Fritz went to get a barrel of gunpowder and some shot that we had left behind. I went to get the butter.

My wife pointed to a bag that I remembered putting into our boat.

"What is it?" I asked.

"Ah!" she said. "That's what I wanted to add to our dinner. Potatoes!"

"There are very few – enough for only one meal," I said,

"but, if we plant them, we'll have plenty next year, enough for all our meals."

Jack was listening to this. "We can eat these potatoes and then we can find wild potatoes, just as you found sugar canes and coconuts."

"No, Jack. Wild potatoes grow on the top of high mountains and they are very small and not very good to eat. These potatoes are very different from wild ones. We must make a garden and grow these good potatoes in it."

"But what can we eat now?" asked Jack.

"I'll see what I can find to use now," I answered, "until our garden is ready. There are some wild plants that we can use instead of potatoes. – Now go with Ernest and try to catch the ducks."

Jack threw little bits of food into the water of the stream and Ernest caught the ducks as they came near to get it.

While they were doing this, Fritz and I went to get salt. The sea water dried on the rocks and left salt behind. We were able to get quite enough to give a taste to our food .... That is what I said: "Quite enough to give a taste to our food," but oh! how foolish we were not to think of more than that!

We went along the stream. The ducks made such a noise that the boys laughed and forgot the heaviness of their load .... They forgot it, but I thought, "Why do we carry these things on our backs and in our hands when there is a much better way of bringing them?"

Chapter 10
The sledge

That barrel of butter was very heavy. I thought, "We must have some way of carrying heavy things."

I thought of our animals tied up at the foot of the tree at night – the donkey, the goats, the cow. We could not tie up the pig. They were not safe. We must make huts for them. These would need wood, far more wood than we had used for the floor of our house; also bamboo. The donkey could not carry so much. We must make a sledge. Those two pieces of wood that I had seen on the shore were just the right shape for the under-part, the "runners", of a sledge.

I decided to take Ernest with me because he is rather lazy, and if there was any danger Fritz would be of greater help to the others. So at first light of day I woke up Ernest and we climbed very quietly down the ladder. I brought a saw and hammer and nails and a piece of light rope.

We found the two pieces of wood. Then we cut cross-pieces and nailed them on to the runners. Then we put a load of bamboo and wood on it. I fixed a rope on the front and we pulled the sledge back along the shore. It ran very well along the sand.

Just as we were finishing our breakfast we heard a great noise among the hens. We all ran.

"It's the monkey!" cried Ernest. "He's following the hens and catching them."

Then we saw the monkey hiding behind a tree and eating an egg. The monkey ran away to another tree and Ernest ran after him. Soon afterwards Ernest came back with four more eggs that the monkey had hidden. My wife went and looked in the grass.

The donkey pulls the sledge to the shore

"One of the hens is sitting on eggs," she said. "Soon we shall have some little ones. We must make a safe yard for the hens and the monkey must be kept away from them."

After dinner, Ernest and I made the donkey pull the sledge to the shore to get more wood and bamboo. While we were loading these on the sledge we set the donkey free. It saw good green grass on the other side of the stream and wandered off across the bridge that we had built.

"It can't have gone very far," I said to Ernest. "Take Flora and bring it back. I want to go for a swim."

I enjoyed the swim very much and when I came back I saw the donkey tied to a tree, but I could not see Ernest. Then I saw him standing on a rock. He shouted to me.

"Look, father! A fish. The biggest fish you ever saw. We must catch it and have it for dinner."

It was indeed a big fish, but how could we catch it? What with?

"Come," I said, "we must go home. There are clouds in the sky and the wind is getting stronger."

Then I looked at the place where the ship had run on to the rocks. There was not much of it left: in another storm it would all be carried away. We must make one more journey to the ship to get some things that we needed. It was our last chance. How could I have been so foolish on our last journey when we brought back the animals? What else did we bring back? Butter, some salt meat, bedclothes, flour, gunpowder, some books. But we knew then that we might have to live on the island for a long time – a year, two years, many years … perhaps for the rest of our lives. What things had we not brought back? Why had I not thought of those other, much more important, things?

Chapter 11
Second journey to the ship

The next morning Fritz and I got up very early and went to look at our boat. It was in good condition, but we had used the sail to make a roof for the Tree House.

"I think," said Fritz, "that we can reach the ship by using the oars. The river will help us on our way."

"Yes," I said, "but we must get another sail from the ship to carry us back when the boat is loaded and heavy. The wind is still blowing out to sea. We'll run back home and tell the others that we'll go now and that we'll spend the night on the ship."

We went quickly and they said that they would meet us when we came back, bringing the sledge to carry our things.

We reached the ship without great difficulty.

"Now, Fritz," I said, "what are the things that we most need?"

"I can only think of a very small thing," he answered.

"What's that?"

"I want a hook to catch that big fish."

"Yes," I said, "that's one of the things. But we can't eat nothing but fish and meat every day."

"No," he answered. "We must have bread, and fruit, and roots and green food."

"We must have what we can *grow*," I said. "You remember Mr Wilkins, on the ship; he was going out to start a home in a new country. He was a gardener. He said that he was bringing some gardening tools. We must find those. Now I'll go down and see if I can find a spade, a fork

31

and other tools, while you go and find a fish hook."

"Yes," said Fritz. "I remember one of the officers was fishing over the side of the boat. I know which his room was: I'll go there and see what I can find."

I went below and was able to find some spades and forks. I hoped to find seeds, but there weren't any. Then I thought, "We must have some seeds. What seeds can we have for growing?... Beans!" I went to the kitchen and found two sorts of beans: I took plenty of each.

Mr Wilkins's room was in the back part of the ship which was now under the sea. We couldn't get any seeds from there, but I thought, "There must be other plants on the island that we could grow for food. If we have beans and potatoes we will be all right."

Fritz came back and said, "I have found a box of fish hooks and string – line, I ought to say – for catching fish."

We found some nets too. They were not very big, but I said, "We can join them together with string. Let's see whether there are any other tools."

We took all the tools that we could find.

"I remember," I said to Fritz, "that Mr Wilkins said that he was bringing a light plough with him. Shall I take the plough to the island?"

"What will pull it?" asked Fritz. "I don't think the donkey can pull a plough."

"No," I answered, "no, I don't think the donkey could pull it, and I don't think a cow and a donkey would work together. But it isn't a very big plough. We'll take it. A time may come when we'll be glad that we brought it."

We slept on the ship that night and waited until midday next day, when the sun was hot and the wind was blowing from the sea to the land. I looked at the sky and I thought that we might have more wind than we wanted because the sky looked rather stormy. We put a good sail on our boat and set out. At first there was little wind and the boat moved very slowly.

"Perhaps," said Fritz, "we can catch a fish on the way back to the land." He put a hook and line over the side, pulling it through the water as we went. Suddenly we felt a hard pull on the fishing line: it was a good thing that we had used the strongest line. The pull was so strong that the boat was pulled backwards.

"The fish is pulling us out to sea," cried Fritz. "It'll carry us away!"

"We must cut the line," I said.

"No, no!" cried Fritz. "Let's wait."

We took our oars and pulled as hard as we could but there was very little wind to help us and we found that the boat was being pulled further and further out to sea.

"I wish the wind would come!" I said.

Just then the wind began to blow and the boat was driven towards the land. The wind blew harder and harder and I thought that the sail might be carried away. We moved faster and faster through the water and at last the boat was thrown up on the land so hard that it broke in pieces.

My wife and the boys were waiting for us there with the sledge. We quickly took our things off the boat and put them on the sledge.

"There! That's all," I said.

"No," answered Fritz. "No! Let's see if the fish is still with us." He went into the water and said, "Yes, it's still here. It's dead." So with difficulty we carried the great big fish on to the land and put it on the sledge.

"This will give us food for many days," I said, "if it doesn't go bad. We must put some of it in salt to keep it."

"But now," said Ernest, "we have no boat. What shall we do?"

"We'll take the barrels that we used for making the boat," I said, "and they'll be very useful for storing food and other things. And, Ernest, you walk along the shore, beyond where the wood was thrown up. I think perhaps one of the ship's boats may have been thrown up."

There was indeed a boat. It was badly broken, but we were able to mend it. So we had a smaller and better boat than the one that we had made for ourselves.

We had some of the fish for supper and it tasted very nice. My wife put aside some of the rest for our meals the next day, and she put some of it into a barrel with salt.

After our evening meal we sat round the fire talking about the things that we must do during the next few days.

"You must make a hut to put the tools and other big things in," said my wife. "You can't carry those spades up and down into our house."

"Yes," I said, "we must also make some huts for the animals, and we must make a garden."

"It must be a big garden," said Fritz. "What have we got? Corn, which we brought from the ship – potatoes, beans. And we may find other plants on the island that are worth growing in our garden."

"That's true," I said. "Yes, but there is more than that. We must make a fence round the garden, or the animals will get in and eat the plants as soon as they come up through the ground."

"Oh, what a lot of work!" said Ernest. Ernest was lazy and did not like work.

"There is one thing you haven't told me," said my wife. "You have told me all the things that we'll be able to eat next year, but you haven't told me what we are going to eat now."

"Ah," I said. "We have no potatoes, but there are plants growing wild which are almost as good. There is the yam. I am sure that there are yams on this island."

Next morning we all went out and looked for yams.

I said, "You will find yams growing where the soil is rather sandy and you will find the plant climbing up some other plant – a small tree, or a cane."

For some time no one found anything. Then Fritz found a plant and he called me: "Is this a yam?"

"Yes," I said. "I think so. Dig down and try to find the root."

Then Ernest called me. "Here's a climbing plant. Is this one?"

"Yes," I said, "I think so. But you must find the root. It is blue or dark red and may be very big. It may be bigger than a football."

Fritz was digging. He said, "I've dug down half a metre but I haven't found any root yet."

"No," I said. "Sometimes the root is a metre down. Go on digging."

Ernest found his root just over half a metre down and was very pleased, and soon after that Fritz found his root. They were both very big roots and we dug them up and put them ready to carry home. We then looked round to see if there were other yams and we found quite a number.

"Well," I said, "we have something which we can use in place of potatoes, and it is also possible to make a sort of bread from yams."

35

Jack had gone further off and he came back and said, "I've found some potatoes, real potatoes."

"No," I said, "potatoes don't grow wild."

"But look at these!" he said, and he showed me the potatoes, green ones.

"Yes," I said. "They aren't the potatoes that we know. They're sweet potatoes: they have green skins and they're very good to eat. We must find as many as we can and plant them in our garden, and use some of them now until we get the others .... Now let's go home."

So we went back to the Tree House.

"First," I said, "we must break up the yams into small pieces and wash them very carefully, because the liquid tastes nasty and is very dangerous. We must wash all the bad taste out of the yam before we cook it."

My wife cooked the yams; they tasted rather like potatoes but not quite so nice. She took some of the yams and made them into a sort of bread. It was rather hard but good.

It was now evening. We had yam bread and some fish for our evening meal.

"When we have dug the garden," I said, "we must go and get bamboo, lots of bamboo. We must make a fence round the garden when we have dug it, and we must make huts for the animals."

"We won't need many huts," said Ernest. "There's only the donkey, the cow, the goats, the sheep and the pig – five very small huts."

"Oh!" I said. "You may soon find that we have many more animals than that."

And indeed I was right.

Chapter 12
Making a garden

We got up very early in the morning so that we could start digging our garden while the air was cool. Fritz and Ernest and I took our spades, and Jack had a fork, though he was not big enough to help very much.

We all set to work, digging. After a time, when we were rather tired, I said, "Let's go and gather the droppings from the places where the animals are tied up at night. We'll bring them to the garden."

After a short time, Jack came running up to me and he said, "The pig! The pig has gone!" It was true: the pig had gone away into the forest.

"Well," I said, "we can't do anything about that. Perhaps she'll come back again."

"You said 'she'?" said Jack.

"Yes, of course. I hope she will soon become a mother pig. Then we shall have a lot of little pigs. I think she has gone away to the forest to have her little pigs there. Then she may come back."

We went back and dug again in the cool of the evening and we were all very tired when it came to the evening meal. We had fish and yams.

"Now," I said, "we must dig again tomorrow, and then we'll get a lot of bamboo and make the fence for our garden and huts for the animals."

"We must make a big hut for the pig," said Jack, "if she has a lot of little pigs. Must we make a big hut for the cow?"

"No," I said, "the cow isn't going to have any little ones. Now, all of you, go to bed and be ready to dig hard tomorrow. On the day after tomorrow we'll go and get the bamboo."

"How will we carry a lot of bamboo over the land? Can the donkey pull as much as we need?" asked Jack.

"No," I said. "We won't go to the place where we got bamboo before. We'll go to a different place and we'll find a much better way of carrying the bamboo to our Tree House."

"Oh?" said Jack. "Is there anything better than a donkey for pulling bamboo?"

"Yes," I said, "there's a much better way. We'll go up the river. We'll cut the pieces of bamboo and pull them to the river and the river will bring them down near to our Tree House."

"Ah!" said Jack. "Yes, that will be the best way."

Chapter 13
Buffaloes

We set off to go and get bamboo to make a fence for our garden and to make huts for the animals. My wife and the four boys came with me and the two dogs, Turk and Flora. We also took the donkey to pull the bamboo to the riverside. Because we were going into country where we had not been before, we took our guns with us. It was a bad thing that we took the dogs – and a good thing that we took our guns.

We went up the river, and we found a lot of bamboo. We cut it and tied it together, and the donkey pulled it to the bank of the river ready to be carried down by the stream. Then we had a meal and rested.

Jack went away and after a time he came back and said, "Father, I've seen a lot of elephants. There is a big open plain over there, and there are ten or fifteen elephants on it."

I said, "Jack, you mustn't say foolish things. There are no elephants in this place. There are elephants in India and there are elephants in Africa, but there can't be any elephants here."

"But there *are* elephants!" he said. "Come and see."

So we all went to see Jack's elephants. When we came out from among the trees I saw a lot of buffaloes standing together.

We went nearer and nearer until we were about forty metres from the buffaloes. They stood and looked at us. I think they had never seen a man before. They did not seem to be angry or afraid, but just stood there looking at us with their big round eyes.

I could see two young ones among the buffaloes. Then Turk and Flora began to jump up and down and make a great noise. At this the buffaloes looked very angry and they came towards us. We were in great danger. The two dogs ran and tried to drive the two young ones towards us, but the other buffaloes ran forward. Then Fritz and I both fired. One of the buffaloes fell dead and the others turned and went away. Perhaps they had not heard gunfire before. We were lucky to escape from this danger so easily.

I said to Fritz and Ernest, "Come and catch those two young buffaloes. We must take them with us."

We went and put ropes round their necks and they allowed themselves to be led away quite easily. We hurried away as fast as the young buffaloes would let us move and went back into the trees.

"Now," I said, "we'll leave the bamboo until tomorrow. We'll come and fetch it then. But we must take the young buffaloes home with us. They are very important! We'll give them milk from the cow."

The cow allowed the young buffaloes to take her milk.

"But," said Jack, "there won't be any milk for us."

"No," I said, "but we can have goat's milk. These two young buffaloes are very important."

"You seem very pleased to have got them," said Ernest.

"Yes, indeed I am," I answered, "because now I can see a way out of two great difficulties."

"Oh," said Ernest, "what difficulties?"

"Well," I answered, "when the cow gives no more milk, that would be the end of milk for us. But these two young buffaloes will grow up, and they will have young ones. So we will have milk for as long as we want, and we will have

We see the buffaloes

41

more and more buffaloes. Buffalo milk is very good. It has a lot of cream in it and we can make butter from it, and perhaps cheese as well."

"And what was the other difficulty?" asked Fritz.

"The other difficulty?" I answered. "You remember the plough that we brought from the ship, and I said that I didn't know what would pull it. A buffalo is very strong and the buffaloes can pull the plough for us. So now we have a plough and we have milk."

"Not yet," said Ernest.

"No, not yet," I answered, "but next year. We must not think only of today. We must think of the years to come, even if our life at present is rather hard."

Next day we went back and cut up the dead buffalo and brought a lot of meat back and put it into barrels with salt so that we would have food in the winter. We also put the bamboo in the river and the river carried it down to a place quite near the Tree House.

We pulled it to the Tree House and set to work making a fence for the garden. Some days later, when this was finished, I said, "Now we must begin to make huts for the animals."

"We will need only four huts," said Ernest.

"Why," I said, "only four huts?"

"Well," said Ernest, "we need a place for the buffaloes and a place for the cow and a place for the goats and a place for the sheep. And perhaps we should make a hen house and a yard for the hens."

"But," I said, "what about the donkey and the pig?"

"Oh," said Ernest, "the pig has gone away. And today the donkey has gone too."

"Gone?" I said.

"Yes. I can't see the donkey anywhere. And the pig went some days ago."

"Yes," I said, "but I hope they'll come back. We'll make huts for all of them, and hope."

We were sitting at breakfast a few days later when Fritz said, "Something is moving among those tall grasses. I'll get my gun." He ran and got his gun.

"Wait!" I said. "Wait! Don't shoot. Let's see what it is."

Jack said, "I'll go and see. I'll go round behind the grasses. I'll find out what it is. If it's dangerous I'll run away."

So Jack moved very quietly. He was very good at moving quietly when he went out shooting birds with his bow and arrow. The thing came nearer and then out came our pig with six little ones!

"Well," I said, "we're all very glad to see you, Mrs Pig. And your house is ready for you. Come along!"

So we drove the pig and her six little ones into the hut that we had made for her. I called Francis.

"Francis," I said, "come and see the pig with her six babies!"

"I have something to show *you*," he cried. "Flora has six babies, too!" And so she had. So now we had eight dogs and seven pigs.

I said, "All we need now is to get our donkey back."

One morning, when we were busy planting potatoes in the garden, we heard a strange noise far away.

"I wonder what that is?" I said. "What sort of animal is making that noise?"

The dogs had heard it too. They made angry noises and looked all ready for battle. We looked all round. We could not see any enemy, but the noise went on. It came nearer and nearer and our dogs became more and more restless. I tied them up.

Then Fritz put down his gun and started to laugh. "I can see it," he said. "That's no enemy. It's our own donkey. He has come back!"

There he was. He came nearer and nearer and then we saw that he had not come back alone. Our donkey was bringing with him another animal, very like a donkey but smaller.

"That," I said, "that must be an onager, a wild ass. It is a beautiful animal and very strong; we must try to catch her. Now," I said to Jack and Ernest, "don't make a sound. Fritz and I will see if we can catch her."

Fritz went forward to our donkey, holding some salt in his hand. Our donkey loved salt. He came up to Fritz and the wild ass came a little closer. Then, when she had got near enough I came from behind and put a rope over her head. She fought against us but at last we were able to tie her up.

I said, "Perhaps the wild ass will have young ones and that will make it easier to teach her and make her useful to us." And indeed that is what happened.

The hens were sitting on eggs, and soon we had forty chicks. So now we had quite a lot of animals to feed. We had the cow, the donkey and the wild ass, two buffaloes, the goats, the pigs and the dogs, the sheep, and the monkey.

I said, "We must work very hard and get food for all these animals because the rainy season is coming."

We brought the tent from the shore and filled it with dry grass. We got sweet potatoes and coconuts and yams, and put them in a dry place at the foot of the tree.

Chapter 14
Preparing for winter

Dark clouds were in the sky. The sea was stormy. The last of our ship had been broken up by the waves and carried away. I thought, "There will be more wood on the shore for us to use, but the sea will be coming up the shore as far as the place where we have left the boat."

"Come, boys," I said, "we must pull our boat high up on the shore so that it won't be carried away by the stormy waves. And we must turn it over so that it won't fill with water."

So we went down to the shore and pulled the boat up high on the sand and turned it over. When we had done that, Ernest pointed and said, "What's that thing there? That square thing." I looked and saw that a box had been washed up on the shore. It was nearly covered with sand. We dug it out and opened it and I saw that it was full of seamen's clothes. This was indeed a lucky find. The clothes were badly spoilt by the sea water.

"But," I said, "we can wash them in the river and dry them."

"They'll be much too big for us," said Jack. "They're too big for Fritz, or Ernest."

"Yes," I said, "they'll be too big for you, but you'll be glad to have them when your other clothes have got wet in the rain."

I thought, "Now winter is coming near, what things do we need? One thing will be dry firewood for my wife to do the cooking under the Tree House." We did not, of course, cook in the Tree House, because of the wooden floor. So we got a lot of firewood and stored that at the foot of the tree under the Tree House. Then I thought, "In the stormy weather we won't be able to go far away from our house to gather food, so let's be sure that we have a good store of food in or near the house, that we can use when the weather is very bad." We had barrels of salt meat, buffalo meat. I hoped that it would keep well, because we could not get any more salt. The waves were coming up over the rocks and there was no hot sunshine to dry out the salt.

We had eggs, of course, from our hens and, with the fishing-line that we had brought from the ship, we might be able to catch fish, though this is not easy when the sea is very stormy. We had yams and we had a lot of coconuts. The goats would give us a little milk – there was no more to be had from the cow. There was plenty of dried grass for our animals.

"Well," I said, "we have a good house and plenty of food, so we are well prepared for the winter."

That is what I thought, but I was wrong – very wrong!

Chapter 15
Winter

I think that the next few months were the most unhappy I have ever known in all my life. We had four enemies – the rain, the wind, the cold and the shorter days. The days were not very much shorter, but we had to spend so much time inside the house because of the bad weather.

The rain came down like a river from the sky. It rained nearly all day and all night, though there were a few days when it stopped. Most of the land was under water and the river was so big that we could not cross it. Our bridge was broken. Luckily our garden was on higher ground and I saw that our plants were beginning to come through.

The wind was very strong. When we made our Tree House I did not think that the wind would blow up into it. If a house is built on the ground and has good walls and a low roof the wind will blow over it, and the house is safe. But with a house built up in a tree, the wind blows up into it. Our roof was made of sailcloth: the rain gathered in it in deep lakes, and great drops came through onto the floor. Then the strong wind came and blew the sailcloth upwards and a river of rain came down into the room.

The days were cooler than they had been and the nights were very much cooler, even cold. We sat all day in wet clothes and we had no way of drying them, and in the cooler evenings we did not know how to keep warm.

We had no fire. We put stones on the floor of our tree room and lit a fire on them, but soon the room was full of smoke and we were afraid that the floor might catch fire. On drier days, the sail that we had used for a roof might also be burnt. We could find no way of getting the smoke

The roof of the Tree House full of water

out of the room. If we made a hole in the roof the rain would come through onto the fire.

When the sun set, darkness came suddenly, but even in the daytime the room was rather dark. We had no light. We had found some waxy beans that we called candle beans; they burned, giving a little light, but not enough to be of any use; so at night we sat round in our wet clothes, very cold, in the darkness, and there was nothing to do but to go to bed.

We could not go on like this.

I said, "We must go down and live at the foot of the tree. We'll spread a sailcloth over this floor, so that there are two roofs – the roof that we have made in the tree and the roof we'll put on the floor here. Then we'll be dry down at the foot of the tree."

We built two walls at the foot of the tree. The animals' huts made the third wall, and the fourth wall was the tree itself. We made a hole in the floor of the upper room to let the smoke from our fire go up into it, so there was no chance of the rain coming straight down on our fire. When we were kept at home all day we spent the time making bamboo mats for the floor.

We were certainly much better in this lower room, but the smell of the animals coming in from one side was almost more than we could bear.

After a time we began to have difficulty with our food. The buffalo meat that we had put into salt in barrels went bad: we had not got enough salt. Oh, why did I not think about how important it was to get salt for keeping food through the bad months of the year? We killed some of the older hens and ate them, and the boys were able to go out fishing or shooting with their bows and arrows when the weather was better. They brought in a little fish and meat. We had yams, but cooking was very difficult. When the weather was good my wife made yam bread, enough to last several days, but it was not very good to eat.

We didn't have enough food for the animals. We killed four of the young dogs, leaving only Turk and Flora and two of their young ones. We had to find food for the cow, the goats, the sheep and the buffaloes. I saw that we could not give them enough in their huts, so we made bells out of coconut-shells and hung them round their necks, and then we turned them out. We put a little food in their huts each night so that they would come home. They went into their huts at night, but in the daytime we sent them out to find food.

Chapter 16
The Cave House

I can hardly tell you how great our joy was when, after those long weeks of rain, the sun shone again and the storms ended. We came out from our dark and smelly room and looked up at the cloudless sky and the bright sun. Around us the grass was green and rich, and flowers were coming through. In our garden, too, the plants were coming up very well. But the birds had discovered this. We put Jack on guard, with the help of Flora, to keep the birds away, and the nets that we had brought to catch fish were also useful in keeping our plants safe from feathered thieves.

We hung up our clothes in the sunlight to dry them, and then we set to work to put the Tree House in order. In a few days we were able to leave our room at the foot of the tree and go back to our bright and happy home.

"Now," said my wife, "we'll be happy – until next winter, when we'll be unhappy again. I can't go through another winter like that. It would kill me. I'm sure that the first men, thousands of years ago, didn't live in trees like monkeys. They lived in caves. We must have a cave."

I knew that she was right. I went out and walked along the shore, looking at the hills facing the sea. Some of them came down almost straight like a wall to the shore. This was the place where I might find a cave. I walked farther and farther, but could see no caves, at least none that was big enough for my family.

I went back and told my wife and the boys that I had not been able to find a large cave, nor any cave which would be of use to us.

"Well," said Fritz, "if the caves aren't big enough, we must dig in one of them and make it bigger."

"You can try," I said, "but the rock is very hard. I don't know whether it will be possible. I'll take you to the best cave I found. It was rather low down on the hill. Perhaps at one time it was made by the sea, but the land has become higher and the sea has gone down and left it there. Bring the tools and we'll see what we can do."

So we went to the cave. We worked for a week, and had only made the cave two metres deeper. The rock was very hard. I thought that perhaps we might make a hole, then put in gunpowder and help ourselves in that way, but I did not want to use a lot of gunpowder. It was too important to us. I didn't know what to do.

"Shall we give it up?" I said to Fritz. "Shall we go on – or think of something else?"

"I think," said Fritz, "that as we go in, the rock becomes a little less hard. This piece here seems softer."

Jack, who was the smallest, had been set to work in the deepest part of our digging. One morning he cried out, "I've done it! I've done it! I've got right through the rock!"

"Don't be so foolish," said Fritz. "You can't have got through the rock with that little bar that you have there."

"But I have!" said Jack. "I have!"

Fritz went to see what he meant. He soon came back, saying, "It's quite true, father. Jack is right. I can't understand it. You can push a bar right through the rock as far as it will go, and there's nothing behind. And I can move the bar about quite easily."

I was very surprised. I took a long bamboo and put it through the hole.

"Yes," I said, "there's nothing behind there."

"Let's make the hole bigger," said Fritz, "so that one of us can go through."

I said, "If one of you goes through that hole, you may fall down a long way and be killed. We must be very careful. Let's make the hole just a little bigger – big enough for me to look in there."

So we made the hole bigger and I put my head in. Suddenly I felt very ill. I drew back.

"Take care, boys," I said. "You mustn't go into the cave – if it is a cave. The air there is bad. It would be certain death to go in there. First we must drive out the bad air."

"How can we do that?" asked Fritz.

"We must light a fire," I replied.

So we put burning grass and sticks into the cave, but the fire went out at once.

"Perhaps," said Ernest, "if we light a fire just in front of the hole, the hot air will draw the cold air out from the cave."

"It might," I said, "it might. But I think it would be very slow and not a very safe way of doing it. I think this is a time when we should use some of our gunpowder and blow the bad air out of the cave."

So I took some coconut shells and filled them with gunpowder and tied string round and round, so as to make a sort of bomb. Then I lit one of these and threw it quickly into the cave. There was a very loud noise and the bad air ws driven out with the smoke. I made two more explosions and then we tried lighting a fire again, and this time it burned. It did not burn well but the smoke and hot air came out through the hole and soon the fire was burning better. At last it was burning brightly, as brightly inside the cave as in the open air.

"Run to the Tree House," I said to Ernest. "Go and

bring all the candle beans that we've got. We can use those to give us a light when we go into the cave."

While he was gone, we made the opening bigger and the daylight came into the cave so that we could see the walls nearest to the doorway. Jack looked in and he said, "It's like a fairy cave. The walls are covered with jewels. It's wonderful!"

I looked into the cave and saw Jack was right. The walls were covered with crystals.

"That's very strange," I said. "Crystals of what? There are crystals of sugar, crystals of salt, and crystals of many other things, and jewels are crystals."

Just then Ernest came back from the Tree House, bringing the candle beans. I went in to the cave first, just to make sure that the air was good. I looked at the crystals. Some had broken off and fallen on the floor because of the explosion. I took one and tasted it. It was salt. – Salt! We would never need to look for it again! Next winter we would have plenty of salt to keep our meat through the bad weather.

It was a very big cave. I saw that we could make a store-room at one end, and a bedroom, and we could have a big room as kitchen and sitting-room.

"But," I said, "there is one thing that we must make at once. I think this end of the cave isn't very far from the outside air. I'll hit the rock inside the cave, and I want you, Fritz, to go outside and listen. Tell me where you hear me most clearly. I'll go *tap-tap*, then *tap-tap*. Tell me where you hear it best, and put a stick to mark the place."

So Fritz went out and I started to hit the side of the cave in different places. After a time he came back and he said, "I've found the best place, I can hear you quite well."

"Ah!" I said. "Then it won't be too difficult to make a hole through there, from the outside air into the cave. It'll be hard work, but we must do it."

It *was* hard work, but after two days Fritz was able to put a bamboo through the hole so that one end of it came into the cave. Then we made the hole bigger from inside the cave.

"Now," I said, "we can make a fireplace, and we can make a chimney. We'll build up some of the chimney outside and we'll make a fireplace inside."

So we set to work using stones and earth, and made quite a good fireplace, and made a chimney outside.

"Now," I said, "we'll see whether our chimney works." So we lit a fire, but the smoke came out into the cave. I saw that the boys were very sad and they thought that all their work was wasted.

"No," I said, "don't worry. When the chimney becomes warm the air will flow up it and it'll be all right. Keep the fire going for two days and you will see that when the chimney becomes warm it'll work very well."

And that was what happened. On the second evening the air began to go up the chimney and to draw all the smoke out of the cave.

"Now," I said, "we need have no fear of the coming winter."

My wife was very pleased. She said, "Now I can cook and dry your clothes and we can sit round a nice bright fire on winter evenings. We'll be very happy."

I could see that there was a great deal more work to be done. The Cave House was some distance from home.

As we walked back to the Tree House in the evening, Ernest was thoughtful and silent.

"What is it, Ernest?" I said.

"It's a long way from the cave to the Tree House," he said, "and in winter we'll have to walk from the cave to the Tree House and back again, twice a day, to feed the animals, to get the eggs, and to milk the goats."

"Ernest is afraid he may get wet," said Fritz, laughing. "Or perhaps he may get tired!"

"Ernest is right," I answered. "It *is* too far. And next winter we'll have many more animals. Have you thought of that? The sheep were very young when we brought them from the ship, but this year they'll have young ones, and the goats will have young ones. And some of the hens will sit on their eggs and we shall have more hens, and more ducks."

"Will we have more monkeys?" asked Jack.

"No," I said. "I think the monkey may go away and have a family with the other monkeys in the forest."

"Oh, no!" said Jack. "Oh, no! He must stay with us."

"Well," said Ernest, "that means that we must make lots more huts and yards at the Tree House, so as to hold those animals."

"No," I answered, "no, Ernest. We must make a farm halfway between the Tree House and the cave, so that it will do for both summer and winter."

"We'll need a great deal more food," said Fritz.

"Yes," I said. "How wise I was to bring that plough from the ship! The buffaloes are growing up and they'll be able to pull the plough. That will be a great help in opening up new fields. We must have corn and potatoes, yams, beans, green plants. To work! To work!"

So we all set to work and we had a very busy summer. We put stores of salt meat, dried fish and coconuts in the cave.

When the end of the year came we stored potatoes and yams. Then we made a storehouse at the farm, and put dried grass and other food in it for the animals. We built a small hut where someone could live and look after them at night and drive away wild animals.

"What are we going to do about clothes?" asked my wife. "The clothes that the boys brought from the ship are nearly worn out and the clothes that we got from the seaman's box are not at all good. They were spoilt by the sea water and are falling to pieces. Perhaps they'll last for another year, but not longer. I must make cloth."

"How can you make cloth?" said Fritz. "From what? We have only got two sheep."

"There are plants," I said, "that cloth can be made from."

I will not tell of all the troubles and difficulties we had with plants for making cloth, but in the end my wife was able to make some. It was not very good and it was not at all white, but she was very happy. But for the present the boys got skins of animals, and, as we now had plenty of salt, they were able to prepare them and my wife was able to make clothes out of them.

So the year passed away – our second year on the island. The boys were getting big and strong. Fritz was now nearing sixteen, and Ernest fourteen. I looked into the years before us. I could see that soon I would have two fine, strong men to help me in our work on the island. As I became older and less able to do hard work, they would be able to take over the work from me. I could see that Jack was a quick learner and was able to help his mother quite a lot, and little Francis, though not very helpful yet, was really a good little boy and gave little trouble.

Chapter 17
Years pass by

As the years went by we were able to make our houses better. We put a wooden roof on the Tree House so that the rain did not come through as it had in our first winter, but it was still not a good home for the rainy season. We also made steps up into it instead of the ladder. We built a room in front of the cave so that we could sit out there and enjoy the sea air and the sunlight. The cave was always rather dark but we used it for sleeping in and one end of it was the kitchen with the chimney. We were able to make a small window on the side of the cave where it was nearest to the outside air.

As the years went by the farm became bigger and bigger. We had buffaloes to do the work of pulling the plough and we were able to make a cart with wooden wheels. It was very heavy but two buffaloes were able to pull it. The buffaloes gave us all the milk we wanted and we were able to make butter for ourselves.

We decided to have no more goats. Goats are very bad animals. They ate the young trees that we planted and sometimes, when they got into our fields on the farm, they undid the work of many days. Two of them escaped and we were afraid that the whole island might be filled with goats and everything very quickly destroyed. So we used the goats for meat.

We got many more eggs from our hens than we could eat in the spring and the summer, but we gave some eggs to the pigs. In the winter we got just enough eggs for our needs. The wild ass had a young one. It was very pretty and it was easier to teach than its mother had been. We had large fields, well fenced, and were able to grow all the food that was needed for ourselves and our animals.

Of course we had troubles. Perhaps the worst thing that happened was when the monkeys came to the farm.

One morning Jack came running back from the farm and cried, "Oh, father, father, come and see!"

I went down there and saw that everything in the farmhouse was thrown about and broken; the fences were pulled up; the growing plants in the fields were beaten down or pulled up and thrown aside. It was as if an army of enemies had come to the place and destroyed everything they could.

I said, "This must never happen again."

Our dogs, Turk and Flora, had had young ones, and these were old enough to be taught. We made it a rule that one of us, Fritz or Ernest or I, would sleep down at the farm with the dogs. They were trained, whenever they saw a monkey, to drive it away. The monkeys came back once or twice, but each time they were driven off, and after a time they did not come any more.

As I watched my boys grow up, I was very pleased with them. They were stronger and bigger than they could ever have been in Europe. Fritz was very strong and tall. Ernest was not so big, but he was quieter, sometimes a little lazy, but he was not so lazy as he had been when a child. He was writing down the names of all the plants on the island and drawing pictures of them. He made some paper out of long leaves, such as the Egyptians had used many thousands of years ago.

Francis was more to be trusted than Jack, though Jack helped a great deal in the work of the farm. Francis helped his mother.

Chapter 18
The canoe

One day Fritz said to me, "I would like to go by myself and find out more about all those parts of the island that we haven't seen. The ship's boat is too heavy for one person to sail. I want to make a canoe."

"Yes," I said, "I think we can make a canoe. I have seen canoes made from the bark of a tree. Let me see if I can help you to do it."

We found a big tree with a good strong bark covering the wood. I cut a ring round the bark down at the bottom, then I fixed a rope ladder to one of the branches and told Fritz to cut round the tree about six metres up from the first place. Then I cut the bark down the whole length between the two circles. We then very carefully separated the bark from the tree. We were afraid that it would break as we were taking it off, but this did not happen. At last the bark fell from the tree in one piece.

We took pieces of bamboo and cane and fixed them into the bark so as to hold it in the right shape. We joined the sides together at each end of the boat and fixed them. We found a sticky liquid which came from a certain tree and which dried quickly. We used this for filling all the places that water might come in.

"I think," said Fritz, "that, as this canoe goes through the water, the water will come in over the front, and perhaps over the back. Perhaps we ought to put a covering over the front and back of the canoe, leaving a place in the middle where I can sit."

"Yes," I said, "You're quite right. We must put a light covering to keep the water out."

We also made a paddle with a flat piece at each end.

When the canoe was finished we left it for some days to dry, and then we tried it in the water. At first the canoe turned over and Fritz fell out rather often.

"It's very difficult," said Fritz, "I can do it when the sea is quiet, but I don't think I could go far if there were many waves."

I said, "The canoe is only good for going in quiet waters, but we must do something about that. I think we should have what is called an outrigger, that is, a bar standing out from the boat with another piece like a little boat at the end."

"That," said Fritz, "will make the boat slower but much safer, but I think with the outrigger I can put a sail in the boat, and when it tries to turn over I will put my weight on the outrigger and so hold it up."

We tried this, and after some days Fritz was able to use a small sail on his boat and to go safely among quite big waves.

Fritz finds the canoe very difficult at first

Chapter 19
Jenny

One day Fritz went off in his little canoe. He was gone the whole day. Evening came and still he had not returned and my wife was afraid that something might have happened to him. The next day we went up to the top of a hill, but we could not see him. Then Ernest pointed. "Look," he said, "that small black thing, very far away."

We looked. It came nearer and we saw that it was Fritz in his canoe. We all ran down to the water to meet him. While he was having breakfast, Fritz told us his story.

"I've always wanted to know more about the land lying to the west. We've never been further than the place where we first came to land years ago, so I decided to go and see. I took my gun and some powder (in a bag to keep it dry), a fish line and my knife. I came to the place where we found shellfish when we first came to land. I went for a swim there, and I found a lot more. I brought some of them up on the shore and opened them. Inside one of them I found this." He held out his hand. In it there was a large pearl. "I opened some more and I found a lot of pearls. Look!" He took from his pocket a handful of beautiful pearls.

"If you make holes through them you can make a string of pearls for mother," said Jack.

"No, no," said my wife, "I don't want them. What could I do with a string of pearls?"

"Perhaps some day," I said, "one of you may wish to go back to Europe and will need money. Perhaps a ship will come which will take you home. These are worth a great deal of money. We'll put them in some safe place."

"I haven't told you the most important thing," said Fritz. "I went on farther into a part of the island where we have never been before. In the evening I sat on the shore and had a meal. As I sat there a big bird flew over. It was flying very slowly and with difficulty. I shot it and when I picked it up I saw why it had been flying so slowly. It had hurt its wing. Then I found a very strange thing."

He showed us a little piece of cloth with writing on it.

"This," he said, "was tied round its leg."

I looked at the writing:

"*Help, Seaman on smoking island.*"

"It looks as if it's been written with blood," I said.

"Yes," said Fritz, "but where was the Smoking Island? I went up the hill behind me and I looked out to sea, and there, far out to sea, there was a little smoke rising into the sky. It came from a small island.

"I went out to the island and climbed up to the top, where there was a little wood, and in it I saw a small hut made of branches. In front of the hut there was a fire with some fish cooking in a big shell. I hid behind a tree and waited. Then I saw someone dressed in a ship's officer's coat come out of the hut. She went to the fire to see how the fish was cooking. I came out from hiding and she turned round——"

"She!" I said. "Did you say 'she'?"

"Yes. It was a young woman! I told her not to be afraid, that my father and mother and brothers had a home about a day's journey away, and they would come and bring her back."

"Yes, indeed we will. But tell me about her."

"Her father is Sir William Montrose, an officer in the army in India. Her mother died when she was born. Her father was going back to England in a ship with his men, so

Jenny had to travel in another ship. The ship was lost in a storm over a year ago. She got away in a boat with a ship's officer and some seamen. The officer gave her his coat and his telescope and told her to keep watch for any other ship or for land. Then another storm came up; a big wave came right over the boat ... and she doesn't know what happened after that. When she opened her eyes she was on that little island."

"How has she lived there for more than a year?"

"I asked her that. She had shellfish. There were some coconuts on trees. She made a fishing-line with her hair and a pin from her dress and caught small fish. She used a glass from the telescope to make a fire. She made a cage for birds out of bamboo, but could only catch small ones. The big bird that I shot had hurt its wing and came down on the island. She tied that piece of cloth with her call for help on its leg, hoping that someone might see it."

"And, by the goodness of God, it came to you."

"Yes," said Fritz. "As soon as I had heard her story I set off at once. I couldn't come all the way home that day, but I slept on the shore and started again as soon as it was daylight ... Can we go to Jenny today?"

"Yes," I said, "yes, if we start at once."

I asked my wife to make everything ready for Jenny. Then, taking a day's food with us, Fritz and I set sail in the ship's boat.

Jenny was standing on the shore waving to us as we came near and, when we stepped out of the boat on to the shore, she threw her arms round my neck and could not speak for tears.

As we sailed back along the shore, Fritz pointed to some of the places that we passed. "There! that's where

65

your bird came down ... This place is where I found a lot of very fine pearls ... Our ship was driven on the rocks here ... We had our tent here ... Here is the mouth of the river. Look up the stream and you can see the bridge. It was washed away in the first winter but we made it stronger. And there ..."He was going to say, "there is the Tree House," but he saw his mother and the three boys waiting on the shore to meet Jenny.

My wife said, "I'll have to dress you just like one of my sons, because these are the only clothes we have."

Jenny, bathed and dressed in seaman's clothes, joined us in a grand dinner, and Jack put a crown of flowers on her head.

Perhaps my boys thought that they would be able to teach Jenny a lot of things, but she could shoot better than they did: "My father taught me in India." She was very good at catching fish. She was able to tell Ernest the real names of many of his plants. "I learnt all that at school." Very soon they were all the closest of friends.

Jenny kept thinking of her father: "If any seamen were saved from my ship they will tell my father where the ship was lost and he will tell ships to look for me."

Then Fritz said, "If a ship comes, the captain may fire a gun, and, if we can answer it, he will know that we are here. There was a small gun on our ship and perhaps we can get it up out of the water from where our ship went on the rocks."

They found the gun and with much difficulty they brought it up to a high point of rock near the Cave House, and they put a lot of wood near it to make a fire and smoke.

"I'm sure that a ship will come some day and take me back to father," Jenny said. "I'm very happy with you, but

Jenny waves to us as we come to get her

he must be very sad, not knowing if I am alive or dead –
always hoping and never knowing."

The weeks passed and the months passed. The summer
ended, and the rains of winter came. Fritz and Ernest lived
on the farm and kept it safe against the monkeys and wild
animals. My wife and I and Jenny and the two younger
boys lived in the Cave House.

The rains ended. The grass became rich and green and
the woods were full of flowers.

Early one morning Fritz went out in his canoe to get a
nice big fish for our dinner. We saw him turn round and
come paddling back as fast as he could.

"Quick! Quick!" he cried. "The gun! There's a ship!"

We ran up to the rocky point and fired the gun, and
Ernest set fire to the wood to make smoke.

"BANG!" There was an answering shot from far away.

We waited, then fired another shot, and the answer
came, louder and nearer.

Then we saw a boat coming towards the shore. We ran
down to meet it. An officer stepped out of the boat.

"I am Captain Littleton," he said, "of the *Unicorn*. I had
hopes of finding Miss Jenny Montrose here. Some of the
seamen from the *Dorcas*, the ship in which she was
travelling, told me that the ship was lost near here."

"Yes," I said, "Miss Jenny Montrose is here, safe."

He looked at me and my family, and at Jenny in
seaman's clothes.

"But . . ." he said.

I told him who I was. "This is my wife . . . my son Fritz
. . . Ernest . . . Jack . . . Francis: and this . . ." I said, ". . . is
Jenny, our Jenny, as much a part of the family as any of my
children."

Chapter 20
The end

It is with a sad heart that I write this chapter.

The *Unicorn's* boat is waiting to take this story of our life here to England, where perhaps it will be made into a book. Others will learn about our beautiful island, and those who love peace and this simple life which has brought us such happiness may wish to join us.

I asked my children if they wished to go back to Europe, or to stay here. Ernest said, "I wish to stay. I shall learn more about the plants, but the captain must send me books."

Jack and Francis were too small to go.

I turned to Fritz. "And you, Fritz? Do you want to go back to Europe?"

He took Jenny's hand in his. "Yes," he said, "we want to go now, but we'll come back."

Captain Littleton left us some much-needed stores and promised to send other things that we needed. We gave him our pearls to sell for us in London to pay for Fritz's schooling and our supplies.

I must stop. The boat is waiting.

Goodbye, my boy. Goodbye, Jenny . . . till we meet again!

Questions

Questions on each chapter

1 *Ship on the rocks*
   1 Who is the narrator – the person who is telling the story?
   2 What did the captain, officers and seamen do?
   3 What useful things did the family find?

2 *The island*
   1 Where did the family land?
   2 How did the narrator make a tent?
   3 What had caught Jack?
   4 What was the animal Fritz found?

3 *The baby monkey*
   1 What did they make from the gourds?
   2 What were the tall grasses they found?
   3 How did they get coconuts?

4 *Back to the ship*
   1 Who went back to the ship?
   2 How did they show that they were on the ship?
   3 Why did they fix barrels to the animals? (To . . .)
   4 Which animal had no barrels fixed to it?

5 *Finding a place for a home*
   1 Why did the narrator's wife want to find a new home?
     (Because . . .)
   2 Where did she want to make the new home?

6 *Going to our new home*
   1 What did they build first?
   2 How did they catch the hens?
   3 How did the hens travel to the new place?

7 *The rope ladder*
  1 What were the sides of the ladder made of?
  2 What was used to make the steps of the ladder?
  3 Who fixed the ladder to the branch?

8 *Building the Tree House*
  1 Who planned the Tree House?
  2 What was the pulley for?
  3 What was the roof of the new house?

9 *Back to the tent*
  1 What did Jack shoot with a bow and arrow?
  2 Why did they go back to the tent? (To get ...)
  3 What did the narrator want to do with the potatoes?

10 *The sledge*
  1 What were the runners of the sledge?
  2 What was the monkey doing?
  3 Why must they make another journey to the ship?
     (To get ...)

11 *Second journey to the ship*
  1 What tools did they want?
  2 What did they find for catching fish?
  3 What happened to the boat?
  4 What could they plant in the garden?
  5 Why did they have to wash the yams carefully?

12 *Making a garden*
  1 What did they want bamboo for?
  2 What would carry the bamboo to the Tree House?

13 *Buffaloes*
  1 What were the "elephants" that Jack saw?
  2 What made the buffaloes angry?
  3 What could buffaloes pull?
  4 What did the pig bring?
  5 What did the donkey bring?

14 *Preparing for winter*
  1 What was in the box on the shore?
  2 What meat did they have in barrels?

15 *Winter*
   1 How much rain fell?
   2 Why was the lower room not perfect? (Because . . .)
   3 Why did they let the animals out in the daytime?

16 *The Cave House*
   1 Who went to look for a cave?
   2 Who found a way through the cave wall?
   3 How did they drive the bad air out of the second cave?
   4 What were the crystals?
   5 What did they store in the cave?
   6 What did they store at the farm?
   7 What two things did they make clothes from?

17 *Years pass by*
   1 Why did they kill the goats?
   2 How did they keep the monkeys away?

18 *The canoe*
   1 What did they need bark for? (To make . . .)
   2 What did they add to stop the canoe turning over?

19 *Jenny*
   1 What did Fritz find inside the shells?
   2 What was on the bird's leg?
   3 Who was Jenny?
   4 What things was Jenny good at?
   5 When did they fire the gun?

20 *The end*
   1 Who went back to Europe?
   2 What did Captain Littleton take the pearls for?

Questions on the whole story

These are harder questions. Read the Introduction, and think
hard about the questions before you answer them. Some of them
ask for your opinion, and there is no fixed answer.

1 What reasons are there for supposing that the island was in the
  tropics – between 23½° North and 23½° South?

2 Choose something from the story to show that the numbered
   statement is TRUE or FALSE (not true) of that member of the
   family. We have done the first one for you to show you the way
   to answer.
   a The narrator (the man who tells the story):
      1 He knows a lot about the world.
         Answer: TRUE. He knew about many things, such as the
                     agouti, gourds, sugar cane.
      2 He never says that he is wrong.
      3 He is a brave man.
      4 He understands his children.
   b The narrator's wife:
      1 She doesn't like hard work.
      2 She is always willing to learn.
      3 She is interested in cooking.
   c Fritz:
      1 He is a hard worker.
      2 He likes a joke.
      3 He doesn't like to be corrected.
      4 He has very useful ideas.
   d Ernest:
      1 He is rather lazy at first.
      2 He is quick to understand how to do things.
      3 He doesn't like to ask questions.
   e Jack:
      1 He is good at moving quietly.
      2 He is a slow learner.
      3 We know more about him than about Francis.

3 What do you notice about the part played in the story by the
   narrator's wife? Do you think she would play a different part if
   the story was about our own time?

4 Which parts of the story do you find easy to believe and which
   more difficult?

5 Do you like the way the story ends? If so, why? If not, how
   would you like it to end?

New words

bark
the strong outer covering of a tree

barrel
a round wooden container for liquids, etc

buffalo
(in this book, the **water buffalo**) a large, grass-eating animal, not unlike the cow in some ways

cane
a tall plant of the grass family; **sugar cane** is such a plant with, inside the hard stem, sweet matter from which we get sugar

canoe
a light narrow boat, moved by a **paddle**

coconut
a very large fruit from a tall tree (a **coconut palm**) that grows in hot countries. Inside the nut-like inner shell there is a liquid ("milk") and sweet white matter

crystal
a regular shape such as salt and some other materials take when they change from liquid to solid form

gourd
a kind of fruit, large with a hard shell, growing on the ground

lobster
a large shellfish which is good to eat but which could hurt someone if it caught a hand or foot

paddle
a short length of wood with a wide part at one end, used like an oar but not fixed to the boat or canoe

plough
a farm instrument pulled (at the time of this story) by an animal or animals. It breaks up and turns over the soil.

pulley
a wheel over which a rope is pulled. It is used to move heavy things.

telescope
an instrument for seeing distant objects, using one eye

yam
a root that grows in hot countries, used for food